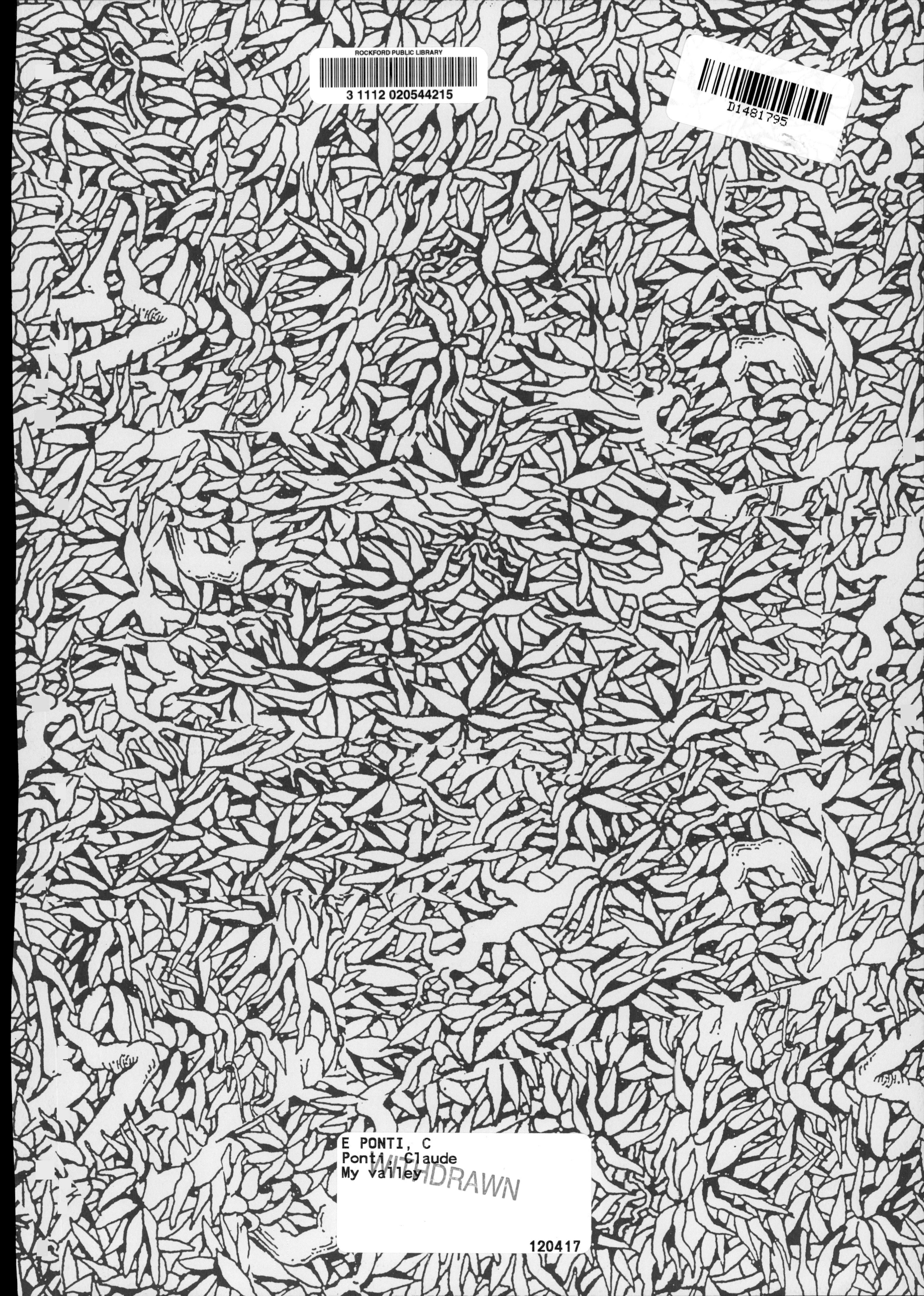
ROCKFORD PUBLIC LIBRARY
3 1112 020544215
D1481795
E PONTI, C
Ponti, Claude
My valley
WITHDRAWN
120417

Original title: *Ma vallée*
Text and illustrations by Claude Ponti
© 1998 *l'école des loisirs*, Paris
English language translation © Alyson Waters, 2017

First Elsewhere Editions Printing, 2017

All rights reserved. No part of this book may be reproduced or transmitted in any form
without the prior written permission of the publisher.

Library of Congress Cataloging-in-Publication Data
My Valley / Claude Ponti ; translated from the French by Alyson Waters.
Other titles: Ma vallée. English
LCCN 2016025390 | ISBN 9780914671626 (hardback : alk. paper)

Elsewhere Editions
232 3rd Street #A111
Brooklyn, NY 11215

Distributed by Penguin Random House
www.penguinrandomhouse.com

This publication was made possible with support from the Lannan Foundation,
the Amazon Literary Partnership, the Nimick Forbesway Foundation,
the National Endowment for the Arts,
the New York State Council on the Arts, a state agency, and
the New York City Department of Cultural Affairs.

Cet ouvrage, publié dans le cadre d'un programme d'aide à la publication, bénéficie de la participation de la
Mission Culturelle et Universitaire Française aux Etats-Unis, service de l'Ambassade de France aux EU.
This work, published as part of a program of aid for publication, received support from the Mission Culturelle
et Universitaire Française aux Etats-Unis, a department of the French Embassy in the United States.

PRINTED IN CANADA

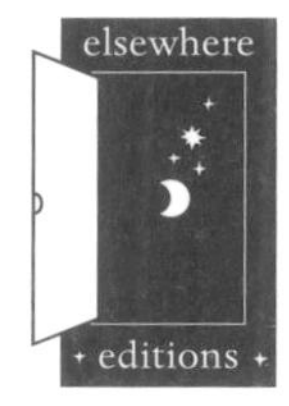

Claude Ponti

My Valley

Translated from the French by Alyson Waters

ROCKFORD PUBLIC LIBRARY

This is my valley. I was born in the House Tree on the Blue Cliffs. I'm a Twims.
All the Twims live in my valley. It's the most beautiful valley in the world.

My Family

When I was born, my mom said: "What a beautiful little Twims. He is soft like the Fluffy-Puffy Island. We'll call him Poochie-Blue." Then she kissed me and my dad put me in his hand and introduced me to the world, the stars, and the moon. He said: "Here is our new child. His name is Poochie-Blue!" The entire world saw me, and I saw that the world was very big, with the sky above, my valley below, and my family in the middle. My family is Dad, Mom, Mom's parents, who always drink their tea sitting on a branch, Dad's parents, who love animals, and my four sisters, my four brothers, and me and my Didi, who is afraid of the rain.

My mom (Mermay-Moom). Sowhatty. Empty-Dempty. Smarghoula. Me. Gussy-Tressy. Bluenote. Boomba-Moomba (below). Olly-Booly (above). Nothin'-Doin' and his Blahblah. And my dad (Bompa-Boom).

My grandparents: Twims Sipoye and Twims Souly, Twims Suziezou and Twims Sibba.

The House Tree

In my house tree, way on top, there is the Star Room where we were all born, except Olly-Booly because Mom was visiting Twims Souly and Twims Sipoye. Way below, among the roots, there are the cellars where the food is stored. Between the two, there are: the bedrooms, a diving board, staircases, the trapeze room, bookshelves, fire in the fireplaces.

House Trees don't grow just any old way. You have to know how to plant them in the right spot and take good care of them. Mine was planted by Pitchy-Patchy Moom, my mother's grandmother's father's grandfather's grandmother. She moved in there when she was two hundred years old, for the birth of her first child, Torn-Beecloo.

LIBRARY
STAR ROOM
SKY
DARK BEDROOM DURING THE DAY
STAIRCASE
BATHROOM
ENTRANCE TO GUEST ROOM
SWINGING BENCH ROOM
LIBRARY
BEDROOM TO SLEEP IN WITH A LOT OF FRIENDS
OFFICE
BEDROOMS
TRAPEZE ROOM
FIREPLACE
SWIMMING POOL
BIG LIBRARY
OUTSIDE
INSIDE
COZY BED TO READ IN
LAMPS
MAIN ENTRANCE
KITCHEN-DINING ROOM
SMALL ENTRANCE
EMERGENCY EXIT
WINTER STOREROOM
STAIRWAY TO THE CELLARS
GROUND

Whenever a Twims makes a wish, he or she goes and sticks a gold leaf on the Singing Stone.
When the wind blows in a certain way, the stone sings and the wishes come true.

It has been this way since the Goochnies' time. The Goochnies are shy and they look like mushrooms.

One day, a long time ago, they disappeared. I always dreamed of seeing a Goochny.
One nice windy evening, I made a wish, and when the stone sang, I saw one.

RED BANK
OTHER POINT
THE THREE BROTHERS
ENDPOINT
ISLAND SEA
FOUNDERS BAY
ISLEPORT
CRANBERRY BAY
COUSIN DUNES
ENDESTPOINT
MAIN ROAD
GATEWAY TO THE ISLANDS
FOREST OF LOST CHILDREN
STROOG'S SANDBAR
CRAZY HAND FOREST
STRAIGHT PATH
PLAYGROUND
SEEKING LOVE WOODS
SALT FIELDS
MUSHY-ROOM FIELDS
SCARY RAPIDS
MARSHMALLOW FIELD
POUTING TWIMS SANDBAR
RESERVOIR
DOUBLE-YOU
SOFT BREEZE FOREST
STARRY DANCER FOREST
FIELD OF GREENS
SINGING STONE
LONELY ROCKS
WORSTEVER FIELD
COW-BLOOCH MINE
BLUE TROUT POINT
ROCK OF TALL STONES
PATH TO PEACE
LOOKOUT ROCK
WAY ABOVE
WAY BELOW
THEATER OF HISSY FITS
BLOOMIN' FOREST
SAND QUARRIES
THE RIVER
HEADLAND WOODS
HEADLAND
NOSY-FINGERED WOODS
GRANT'S ARMCHAIR
TROMBE BEACH
HISSY FIT PATH
MIDDLE MARSH
PI PI PINE
VEGETABLE GARDENS
CHORAL REEF
WHISTLING BULLRUSH PLAIN
O'GHOUL SANDBAR
WHIRLWIND FOREST
TREE OF SECRETS
COULD BE
FOREST OF THE LAUGHING TWIMS
GREEN BEAN LANE
BROKEN HEART
TREE OF FRUITS
DAD'S NIGHT STATUE
MYRVE
POSTMAN'S PATH
ROCKY ROAD
SLONG PLAIN
WEEPY RAVINE
CUBBY HOLE
MEATY WOODS
PLAIN
WINDY PATH
STONE BRIDGE
LONGEST WAY
PATH ROAD
MUSHROOMY WOODS
WOODS OF TEARS
GREEN KNEE FOREST
CEMETERIES
THE GREEN
MELON-COLLY WOODS
FOREST OF GARDENS
HERE FELL THE CHILDREN FROM THE SKY
TOOM CROSSROAD
MY PLACE
HOLE WOODS
HOLE BRIDGE
PATH TO THE SKY
EGG PLAIN
GOOCHNY POND
GOOCHNY BRIDGE
BLUE CLIFFS
PITCHY-PATCHY MOOM'S FIR FOREST
WOODS OF THE POND
ALONG-THE-WAY
POTTED WOODS
NAPPING WOODS
BIG WATERFALL
LITTLE WATERFALL
BRIDGE OF THE WOODS
BEECH WOODS OF THE POND
MY FAMILY'S HOUSE TREE
WINDING PATH
BLUE CLIFFS
THE LAND BEHIND

The Forest of Lost Children

When Pitchy-Patchy Moom was alive, Piong, a young child, got lost in a forest. He came out three hundred years later, a little bit bigger. His family was as happy as he was when he returned. Today, the children play at getting lost in the forest. They are not afraid because Blowakiss, Piong's daughter, found an easy way to come back.

To play the game, every child gets a string. You mustn't lose it. You can see the Well of Stars, then follow Piong's tracks and pass in front of the Sleeping Monster. No one knows how to wake up this monster. But no one tries. We don't know if he's nasty or nice.

Sometimes, a storm will come. If we are out on the Blue Cliffs right before it breaks and we turn around, we can see the Land Behind. And go there. The painter Ootsomay-Song went there.

He said it was deserted. Uninhabited. It's strange to think that right behind my valley there is another country where no one lives. Absolutely no one.

Other times, in the morning, the fog covers the entire valley. It's warm out and you can't hear a sound. The Blue Cliffs turn blue. It's as if a secret appears.

For my secrets, I go inside the Tree of Secrets. And I whisper in his ears.
He's a mute tree. He never repeats what you say to anyone.

The Children Who Fell from the Sky

One day, a very strange House Tree moved through the sky. It had been uprooted by a hurricane; you could see its roots. Children fell from it. Three children who looked exactly like Twims, except they made a little spark when you touched them. Lu-Gong kept an eye on the sky from Lookout Rock. But that House Tree never came back this way. So the children who fell from the sky adopted a family. Every family dreamed of having them. These children also had Floataboat Tree seeds in their pockets that no Twims had ever heard of before.

The spark from the children of the sky didn't work after a year.

The first Floataboat Trees.

"Hurry! We can't let children fall like that!"

The Very Sad Giant

It happened one day when I was alone with my sister Smarghoula. A Giant came into the Valley. He had never seen a House Tree. He didn't know what it was for. Because he was much too big to go in, he was sad. The third time he came to peek in through the door, he sat down and didn't budge. He wanted to know. Smarghoula said: "Okay, we'll show you." For three days and three nights and one morning we showed him. We went to get everything we could and showed him how we used it all. We explained the doors, windows, and stairs to him. We slept, yawned, ate, drank hot chocolate,

made sandwiches, read books, we washed, woke up, bathed, cooked meals, did the dishes, made fires in the fireplaces, played games, made tea, and lit lamps. In the end, he said: "I get it, I'm going to make a House Tree in my valley." And he left and never came back.

On some days, I climb up to the Observatory. I sit on

the edge of the very last rock and look out at the sea…

Winter

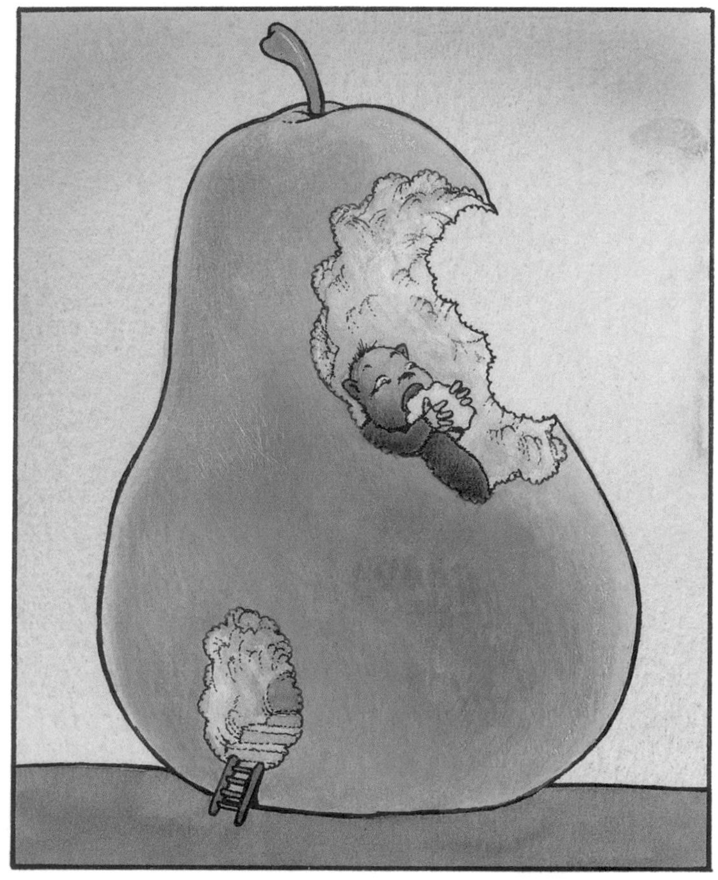

As soon as it snows, we have a snowball fight. It's the best way to make snowmen who look like us. Eating can be fun, but not for long. We can also dance with a young Floataboat Tree to get it used to waves. I like to watch TV, but I like putting on shows even more. I also like to race on the frozen river. Especially when I am out in front of everyone else and can't see them anymore because they are so far away.

But what I like best is when we all get together to read stories in books.

The Big Wind and the Middling Wind

When the Middling Wind blows, we scatter all over the Valley. The first person, the one who is the farthest away, tells a story. When the wind carries it to the second person, the story is already different. The second person tells it in turn, and the wind changes it again...

Sowhatty made a cherry pie and hid it 'neath her bed.
I trusted her so tasted it, then ate it all alone.
Sowhatty made a berry cry then spit under her bed.
Disgusted, she said "I hate it" at the old tailor's home.
Coyote saw a merry cat with a wreath upon his head
He said, "Take off that silly hat and kindly use a comb!"
The spaghetti turned an eerie green, but the tomato sauce stayed red.
"I'll eat some though it's hairy but will NOT write a poem."
Bluenote caught a fairy queen so sang a song instead
Of going to the dairy to drink the creamy foam!

It's been a long time since Switchy-Blue let himself go in the Big Wind. He wanted to live with the birds. From time to time, the Twims could see him sail by in the sky. One day, they noticed a feather growing out of his head and he wasn't happy about it. Lu-Gong decided to save him.

He climbed up to the top of the Tree of Fruits looking for the perfect moment, and grabbed him. And that's how Switchy-Blue was saved by Lu-Gong.

The Cemetery

Whenever a Twims dies, we bury him in the cemetery in his garden. Exactly the garden he wanted. There's the garden of the Twims who loved the mountains. And the Twims who longed to be a Pine tree. And the Twims who hated everyone. Gardens for serving tea, collecting mushrooms, or picking flowers. The garden of the notebook to write a bit of a story in as you go by, for the Twims who loved to read.

The garden of eggs made of stone. The garden of fiery eyes. The garden made for lovers to kiss in.

The garden to pine for from afar.

The garden that sings and rings.

The garden of the Twims that liked to hear children playing.

The garden of the never-ending story.

The garden-palace of the person who's waiting for the Goochnies to come back.

The Islands

It was Twisty-Bun, a child who fell from the sky, who was the first to sail on a Floataboat Tree. It was better than our little walnut boats. We could finally go very far away. No Twims has yet to discover the place where the sea ends, but we found out how it fills up. It's at Bathtub Island. (Foodurday-Too's third expedition.) The water runs continuously and makes the foamy mousse we eat for dessert. It changes flavor every season.

Twims Sitooly-Bun, who has twenty-seven grandchildren, said that there are as many islands as there are stars. The best known are: Softy Sleepy Island and its Storytelling Pillows, Mushy Island, which is

completely edible, Fluffy-Puffy Island, and Surprise Island, where you find a new present every day.

COUCOU

The Theater of Hissy Fits

If a Twims is really angry, he or she goes to the Theater of Hissy Fits. One time, for example, I was very angry with Tornik-Orge. He had broken my push puppet, Tootoo. By the way Tornik-Orge's ears were folded, I knew he had done it on purpose. I went to the Theater. In the workshop, I made a Very Angry Mask and a marionette that looked just like Tornik-Orge, with his idiotic expression. After, I went on stage and threw a Big Hissy Fit. I said everything I was thinking and even things I didn't know I was thinking. I shouted, screamed, stamped my feet, punched and hammered. I smashed the marionette to smithereens. And the smithereens asked my forgiveness.

The Rain

My favorite game when it rains is looking for the Magic Puddle. Among all the puddles in the Valley, there is only one Magic Puddle each time it rains. It's the only puddle where you can go in and then come out through any other puddle. All the other puddles are exits. It's so much fun once you've found it to dive in without knowing where you'll come out. I also like to go catch the Up-in-the-Skies that grow really fast during rain showers. You can do lots of things with them, including looking for islands.

I like to take the young Floataboat Trees out for a walk to water them, but I don't like to take care of the rain catcher very much. I know that the best tea can be made with morning rainwater, but it's a game where you don't move at all. All you do is wait.

The King of Trees

The King of Trees is called O'Mess-Messian. He loves listening to the birds sing. His head is full of birdsong. He makes his branches grow in special ways so that they can hold as many nests as possible. When he feels like changing music, he simply changes forests. It's very unusual for him to move in daylight. Olly-Booly saw him. I never did. Ever since he found out that books are made from trees, O'Mess-Messian dreams of the book he will become one day when his life as a tree is over. He would like it to be a very beautiful book. Sometimes he even wonders if he isn't going to write it himself.

When O'Mess-Messian wants to hear the birds, he shakes his head.
The birds fly all around for a little while, then land again on his branches and start to sing.

Summer

It's in summer that the Tree of Fruits is the most magnificent. It's covered in all kinds of fruit. That's why Pitchy-Patchy Moom had planted our House Tree right next to it. In summer, we play a lot. During the Festival-of-the-Shortest-Night, we don't sleep, we taste all the fruit, and we dance around a fire. The bravest Twims jump across it. (I did it five times.)

In summer, I tell him my secrets.

Dads' Night

Lots of times in my bed I've wondered what parents do at night. I slept. But what did they do? Whenever I thought about it, it would wake me up. One night, it woke me up so much that I got out of bed. I went to see what my dad was doing. He was leaving the House Tree. I followed him without making a sound until we came to a statue I had never seen. He went inside it. When he came out, he caught me. He said: "Fine, come along, you're big enough now, I'll explain everything to you..." The two of us walked and he explained everything to me. That particular night was Dads' Night. It only comes once a year. A big statue of Dad Twims appears on the mountain. And all the dads go inside it to learn how to be a dad. After a while, we sat down and watched the statue disappear. Then we went home. I asked if there was a Moms' Night, too. He said there was, but it was a Moms' secret. When I went back to bed, I asked myself: "And children"? My Didi answered me: "Every night is Children's Night for children." That's the only time my Didi ever spoke.

Twims Sou-Loussouf, who lived until he was one thousand two hundred forty-seven years old, said: "Our valley is like the Doll House Tree in the Twims' House Tree." I don't know if it's true, but if my valley is a teeny-tiny valley in a bigger valley, then one day I'll go see.

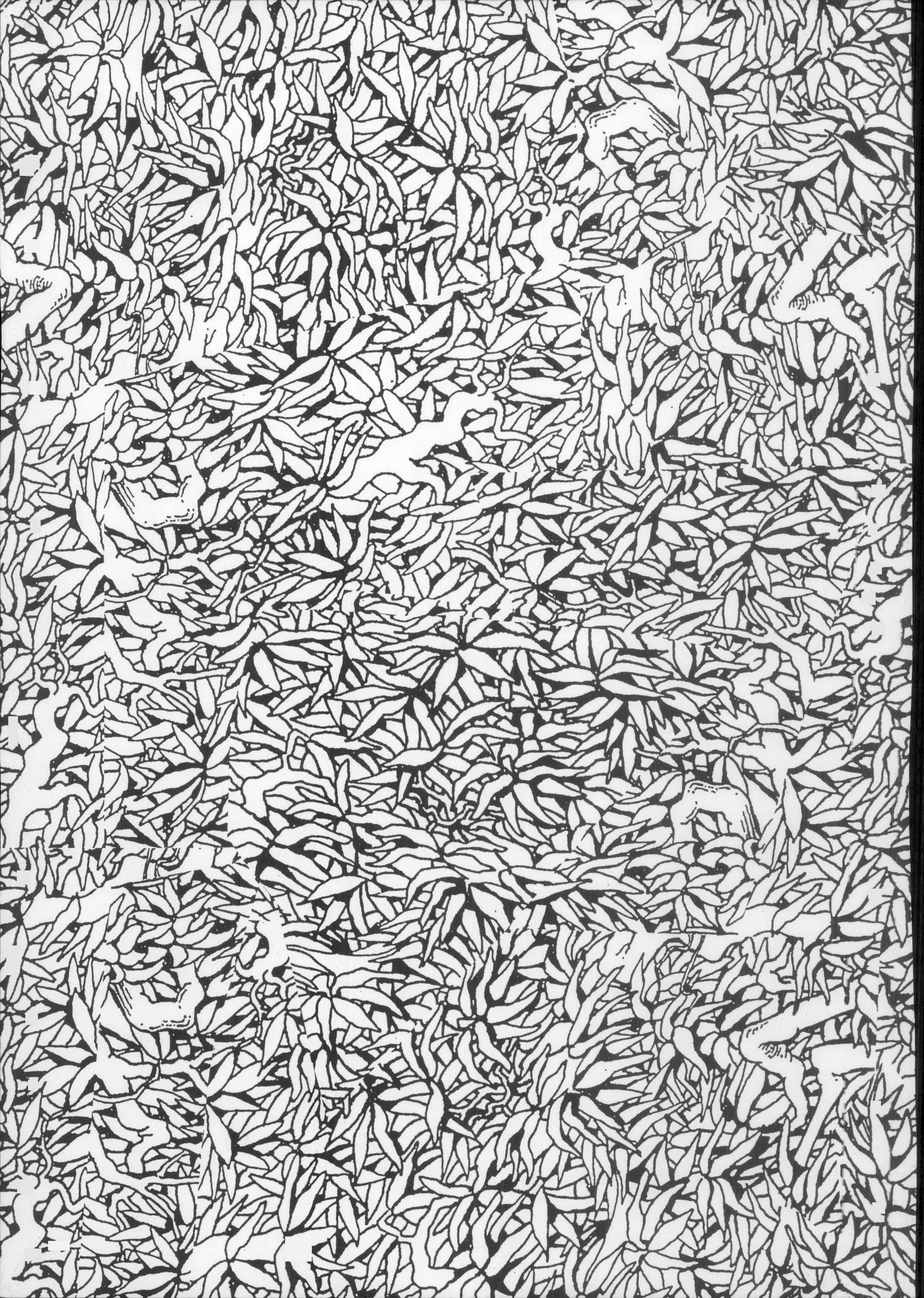